ATOMIC BOMB PERSPECTIVES

THE MANHATTAN PROJECT

BY RYAN GALE

CONTENT CONSULTANT
Allan M. Winkler
University Distinguished Professor of History (Emeritus)
Miami University of Ohio

Cover image: Physicist Norris Bradbury stands next to a test atomic bomb in 1945.

Core Library

An Imprint of Abdo Publishing
abdobooks.com

abdobooks.com

Published by Abdo Publishing, a division of ABDO, PO Box 398166, Minneapolis, Minnesota 55439.

Printed in the United States of America, North Mankato, Minnesota
052021
092021

THIS BOOK CONTAINS RECYCLED MATERIALS

Cover Photo: Science Source
Interior Photos: AP Images, 4–5, 8, 32–33, 35, 43; Gritsalak Karalak/Shutterstock Images, 10; Everett Collection/Newscom, 12–13; Unknown Agence Quebec Presse/Newscom, 16; Los Alamos National Laboratory/Science Source, 18–19; CSU Archives/Everett Collection/Newscom, 20; Corbis Historical/Getty Images, 23, 45; Claus Lunau/Science Source, 25; Ed Clark/The LIFE Picture Collection/Getty Images, 26–27; Galerie Bilderwelt/Hulton Archive/Getty Images, 39

Editor: Maddie Spalding
Series Designer: Ryan Gale

Library of Congress Control Number: 2019954297

Publisher's Cataloging-in-Publication Data

Names: Gale, Ryan, author
Title: The Manhattan Project / by Ryan Gale
Description: Minneapolis, Minnesota : Abdo Publishing, 2022 | Series: Atomic bomb perspectives | Includes online resources and index
Identifiers: ISBN 9781532192685 (lib. bdg.) | ISBN 9781098210588 (ebook)
Subjects: LCSH: United States. Army. Manhattan Project--Juvenile literature. | Atomic bomb--United States--History--Juvenile literature. | Weapons of mass destruction--Juvenile literature. | Military history--Juvenile literature.
Classification: DDC 623.45119--dc23

CONTENTS

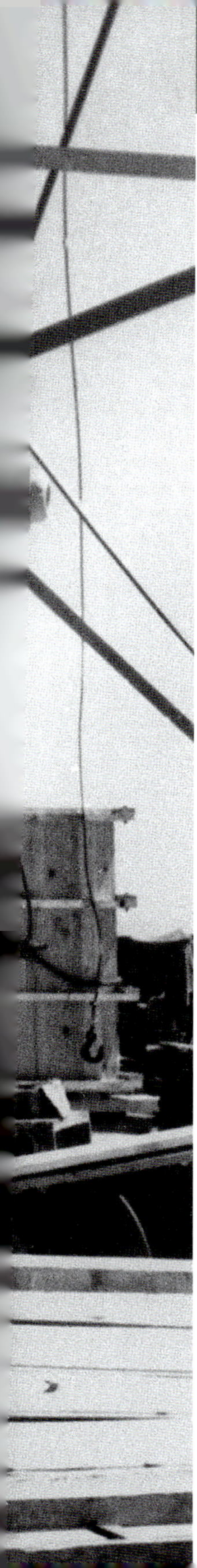

CHAPTER ONE

CHAIN REACTIONS

On July 16, 1945, an atomic bomb exploded over the desert in Alamogordo, New Mexico. An atomic bomb is a powerful weapon. It explodes when atoms in the bomb split and release energy. The bomb that day held only 14 pounds (6 kg) of atomic material. But its blast was as powerful as 21,000 tons (19,000 metric tons) of explosives. The light from the blast was brighter than the sun. A mushroom-shaped cloud stretched miles into the sky.

Workers raised the test bomb high up in a tower so it could explode in the air like the real bombs would.

The explosion left a crater 1,000 feet (300 m) wide and 10 feet (3 m) deep. But no one was harmed. It was just a test. The test was part of the Manhattan Project. This project involved the building of the atomic bomb. The Manhattan Project was top secret. The United States hoped the bomb would help end World War II (1939–1945).

The United States had entered the war in 1941. It fought alongside Great Britain, the Soviet Union, and China. These countries were the Allied powers, or the Allies.

PERSPECTIVES

WATCHING THE TEST

A group of scientists and engineers watched the atomic bomb test. They had helped build the bomb. They stood miles away from the bomb during the test. They wore goggles and covered their skin as a precaution. Some people worried that the explosion might be more powerful than they had predicted. Val Fitch was a physicist who saw the test. He said, "It's hard to overstate the impact on the senses of something like that. First the flash of light, that enormous fireball, the mushroom cloud . . . and then, a long time afterwards, the sound. The rumble, thunder in the mountains."

They fought against Germany, Italy, and Japan. These countries were the Axis powers. By mid-1945, Japan was the only Axis power that had not surrendered. US officials decided to use the atomic bomb against Japan. They hoped this would push Japan to surrender.

LEO SZILARD

Physicist Leo Szilard heard about the test's success while at his laboratory in Chicago, Illinois. Szilard had helped work on the bomb, but he had mixed feelings about it. He knew it could help the Allies win the war. But he was concerned that it could be used to harm innocent people.

Szilard grew up in Hungary. He later studied engineering and physics in Berlin, Germany. But he moved to England in 1933 to escape persecution. He was Jewish. Adolf Hitler, the leader of the Nazi Party, had just taken over Germany. The Nazis believed that Jewish people were inferior to them. They targeted

Szilard became a US citizen and moved to New York in 1940.

and oppressed Jewish people across Europe. They later killed millions of Jewish people during World War II.

While working in England, Szilard studied atomic chain reactions. In this process, neutrons are released from splitting atoms, and they go on to split other atoms. This chain reaction releases a type of energy called radiation. Szilard knew this process could be useful. It could power cities. But there were also risks. It could be used to make powerful weapons.

AN URGENT LETTER

Szilard eventually left England and moved to the United States. In 1939, he learned that German scientists had split a uranium atom by shooting neutrons at it. Uranium is an element. This means it is made from a single type of atom. Splitting a uranium atom releases radiation. This was the first step in creating a chain reaction. The German scientists called this process nuclear fission.

NUCLEAR FISSION

An atom is made up of different parts. Particles called electrons orbit a nucleus. The nucleus contains proton and neutron particles. The nucleus can split when hit by another neutron. When this happens, the two nuclei take some of the electrons with them. They form two new atoms. This process is called nuclear fission. Energy is released during the fission process. When an atom splits, it also gives off extra neutrons. These neutrons can split other atoms, causing a chain reaction. This releases a tremendous amount of energy.

Szilard was afraid the Germans would use uranium to build a weapon. So he sent a

ATOMIC CHAIN REACTIONS

An atom has a central part called a nucleus. The nucleus is made up of particles called neutrons and protons. The first atomic bomb contained a certain type of uranium atom. This diagram shows how the uranium nuclei split to create a chain reaction. Does this image help you better understand the process? Why or why not?

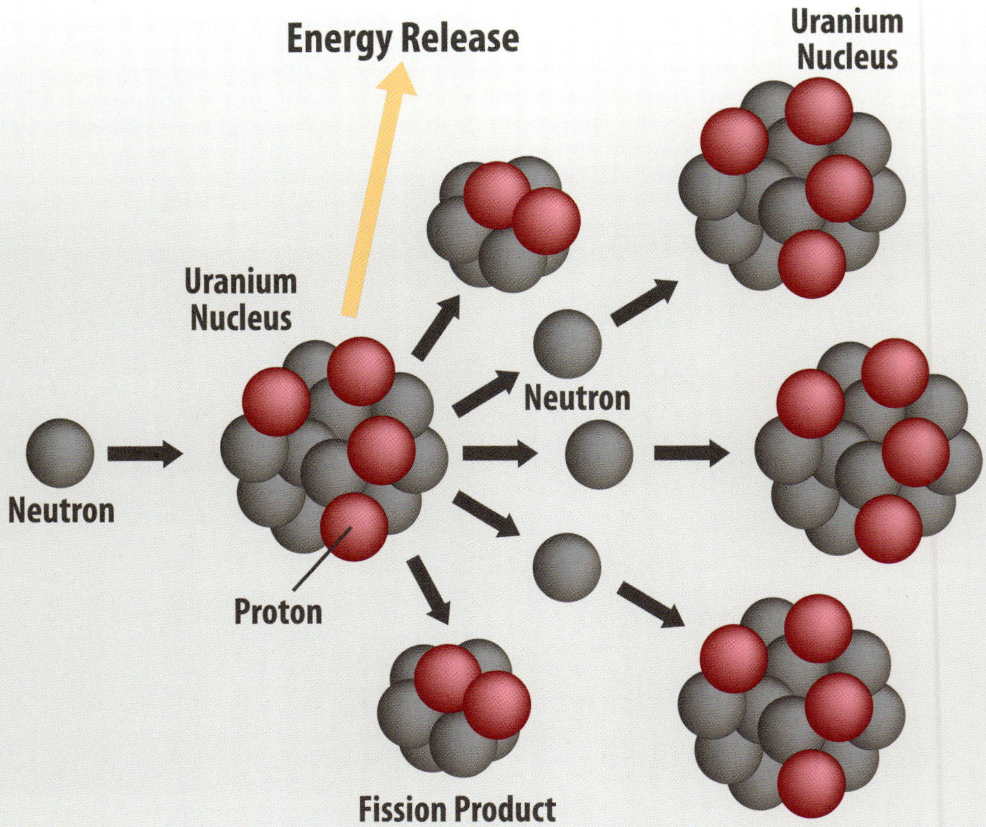

letter to the president of the United States, Franklin D. Roosevelt. He urged Roosevelt to take action.

Roosevelt read Szilard's letter shortly after Germany invaded Poland on September 1, 1939. This invasion was the start of World War II. Roosevelt knew the Germans wanted to take over the world. So he took the German threat seriously. In response to the letter, he created the Advisory Committee on Uranium in October. The committee confirmed that uranium could be used to build an atomic bomb.

FURTHER EVIDENCE

Chapter One describes the world's first atomic bomb test. What was one of the main points of this chapter? What evidence supports this point? The article at the website below gives more background on this subject. Find a quote on this website that supports the point you identified.

THE FIRST ATOMIC BOMB TEST

abdocorelibrary.com/manhattan-project

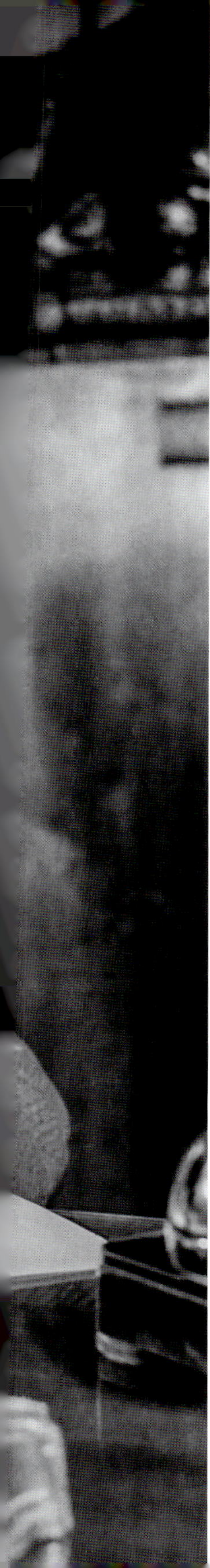

CHAPTER TWO

FROM RESEARCH TO DEVELOPMENT

Thousands of people worked on the Manhattan Project. Vannevar Bush was one of them. He was an engineer and inventor. He was also the vice president of the Massachusetts Institute of Technology. He thought civilian and military scientists should work together to research new military technology. In June 1940, Bush told Roosevelt about his idea. Roosevelt agreed. He created the National Defense Research Committee (NDRC). Bush was made chairman

Vannevar Bush oversaw approximately 6,000 scientists as head of the NDRC.

of the committee. The NDRC researched many subjects, including atomic energy. At the time, most atomic research was being done by civilian scientists. They worked at universities around the country. The NDRC helped military and civilian scientists work together. But it did not have the funds to develop new technology.

PERSPECTIVES

BRITISH CONTRIBUTIONS

Great Britain began an atomic bomb program in 1940. The group that worked on this program was called the Military Application of Uranium Detonation Committee. This group shared its research with the United States. Great Britain later sent scientists to work on the Manhattan Project. The group was known as the British Mission. These scientists' efforts helped the project advance quickly. Physicist Hans Bethe worked with the British scientists. He wrote in 1949, "The collaboration of the British Mission was absolutely essential."

In June 1941, Roosevelt established the Office of Scientific Research and Development (OSRD). The NDRC became part of this group. The OSRD researched and developed new military technology. Bush became the OSRD's director. The atomic program grew quickly under the OSRD's control.

ISOTOPES

Each atom in an element has the same number of protons and electrons. For example, each uranium atom has 92 protons and 92 electrons. But the number of neutrons in an atom can vary. Each variation is called an isotope. Uranium has three natural isotopes. Several more can be created in a laboratory. The uranium-235 isotope is needed to fuel a bomb. But it makes up less than 1 percent of the uranium found in nature. Scientists needed large amounts of this isotope to make a bomb.

PEARL HARBOR

On December 7, 1941, the Japanese military attacked a US naval base in Pearl Harbor, Hawaii. The United States declared war on Japan the next day. Soon after, Germany and Italy declared war on the United States. After these events, the US government decided to build an atomic bomb. It thought a bomb might help the Allies win the war.

The Pearl Harbor attack killed 2,335 military personnel and 68 civilians.

Bush needed to build factories to process uranium. But the OSRD did not have enough resources to do this. Bush met with government officials in mid-December. They agreed that the US Army should take over the atomic program. The army could handle large engineering and building projects. But it would take several months for the army to arrange the takeover.

A SECRET LABORATORY

In late 1942, Italian physicist Enrico Fermi became the first person to create an atomic chain reaction.

Fermi worked at the University of Chicago's Metallurgical Laboratory. This site was more commonly known as the Met Lab. The Met Lab was the OSRD's new secret atomic research center. Scientists from across the country came there to work. Chemist Glenn Seaborg was one of these scientists. He had discovered plutonium in 1940. He learned that plutonium would make a better bomb fuel than uranium. But Bush was not ready to abandon uranium. He chose to move forward with both uranium and plutonium production.

EXPLORE ONLINE

Chapter Two talks about engineer Vannevar Bush. The website below also has information on Bush. As you know, every source is different. How is the information from the website the same as the information in Chapter Two? What new information did you learn?

ATOMIC HERITAGE FOUNDATION: VANNEVAR BUSH

abdocorelibrary.com/manhattan-project

CHAPTER THREE

A SECRET PROJECT

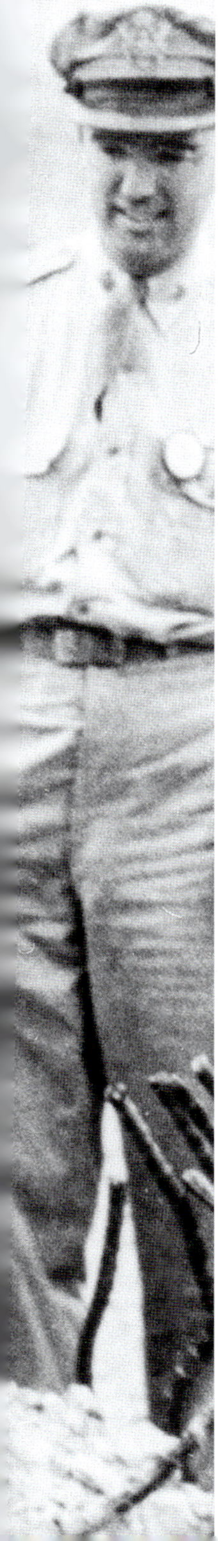

The US Army took over the OSRD's atomic bomb program in August 1942. The army created a new district to manage the program's construction needs. There were already 11 military districts throughout the country. Each district was in charge of military construction projects. The new district would oversee the building of labs, factories, and other construction projects related to the bomb program. Colonel James Marshall became the district's director.

General Leslie Groves, *center*, looks at the ruins of a tower after the atomic bomb test in 1945. Groves led the Manhattan Project from September 1942 to 1946.

Groves was an engineer who helped build the Pentagon, the office building for the US Department of Defense.

The district's main office was in Manhattan, New York City. The atomic bomb project became known as the Manhattan Project.

GETTING STARTED

Marshall stepped down as director in September 1942. General Leslie Groves replaced him. One of Groves's first jobs was to begin producing atomic fuel. An atomic bomb needs a lot of fuel. Groves believed several of these bombs would be needed to win the war. So he had to build factories that could produce large amounts of fuel. He looked around the country for places to build the factories. He sought out remote areas where people could work in secret.

Groves purchased land near the town of Clinton, Tennessee. The army built factories there to process uranium. The army gave the site the code name Site X. It was publicly known as the Clinton Engineer Works. This made it sound less suspicious. People who worked there called it Oak Ridge after the name of a nearby hill.

In November 1942, Groves bought a second site in Los Alamos, New Mexico.

FORCED OUT

The land Groves bought for the Manhattan Project was not uninhabited. Approximately 3,000 people lived on the Tennessee site. More than 2,000 people lived in and around Hanford. There was a boys' school on the site in Los Alamos. Everyone who lived in these areas had to move. Groves paid people for their land and houses. Most were not happy with the deal, but there was little they could do.

The code name for this place was Site Y. Workers built an army base there with a secret bomb-production lab. The lab was called the Los Alamos National Laboratory.

Groves later bought a third site near Hanford, Washington. Its code name was Site W, but it was publicly known as Hanford Engineer Works. The army built a plutonium production center on this site.

BUILDING BOMBS

Scientists and engineers at Los Alamos had soon designed a bomb. The bomb acted like a gun, firing one mass of atomic fuel at a second mass. The impact would start an atomic chain reaction. The result would be a large explosion. But this method would not work with plutonium. Firing plutonium at high speeds caused it to melt. An implosion method would have to be used for a plutonium bomb. This method involved directing a series of explosions inward toward a ball of plutonium.

The Manhattan Project team built two different bombs over the next two years. The finished uranium

People who worked at the Los Alamos National Laboratory had to wear gloves and follow special safety rules because they worked with dangerous materials.

bomb was 10 feet (3 m) long and 28 inches (70 cm) wide. The team called it Little Boy. The plutonium bomb was slightly longer and twice as wide as the uranium bomb. The team called this bomb Fat Man.

SELECTING TARGETS

On May 7, 1945, the German army surrendered. But the Allies were still at war with Japan. The Manhattan

Project's Target Committee thought about where to drop the bombs. The committee had originally focused on bombing Germany. After Germany's surrender, the committee switched its focus to Japan. It considered many Japanese cities, including Hiroshima and Kokura. There was a Japanese military base in Hiroshima. Kokura had one of the country's largest weapons factories. The committee chose other cities as alternate targets. One was the city of Nagasaki, where Japanese warships were built.

PERSPECTIVES

WAR IN THE PACIFIC

The war with Japan was long and difficult. Japan had a powerful navy and air force. Japanese soldiers were stationed on many islands in the Pacific Ocean. The fighting on the islands took the lives of many US soldiers. The US military considered invading mainland Japan as a way to end the war. But this action would have cost many lives on both sides.

HOW THE BOMBS WORKED

This image shows how the two types of atomic bombs worked. Fat Man was a plutonium bomb. Little Boy was a uranium bomb. What were the advantages of building two types of bombs? What challenges might scientists have faced while working on these bombs?

FAT MAN

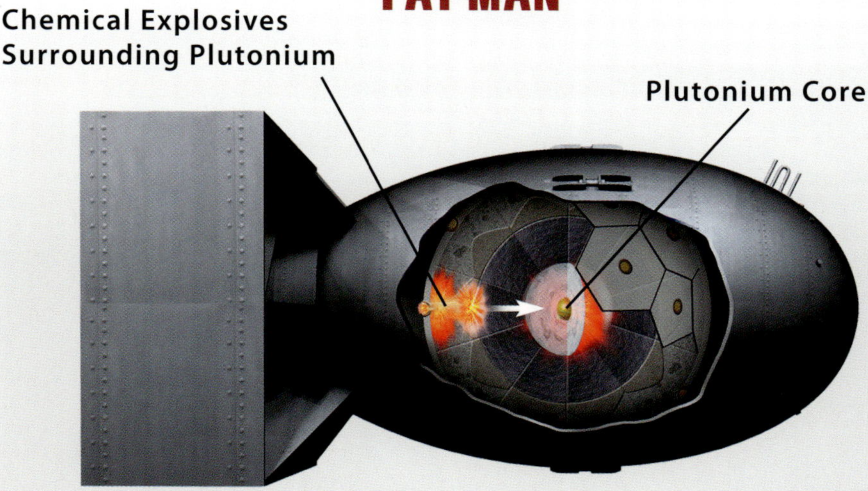

LITTLE BOY

CHAPTER FOUR

THE WORKERS

The army hired more than 125,000 people to work on the Manhattan Project. Some were scientists and engineers. Others were teachers and nurses. Teachers educated the workers' children. Nurses treated the workers and their families. People were eager to work on the Manhattan Project. They wanted to contribute to the war effort in any way they could.

Most of the people who worked on the project had to move to the remote

Manhattan Project employees at the Oak Ridge site leave work at the end of the day.

WOMEN IN THE WORKFORCE

Hundreds of women worked on the Manhattan Project. Female scientists worked in Los Alamos and at the Met Lab. Some were human computers. They solved difficult math problems. Others worked in hospitals, offices, and schools in secret cities. Female soldiers from the Women's Army Corps (WAC) also worked at each site. The WAC was part of the US Army. These women were technicians and secretaries. They often handled top-secret information.

project worksites. Engineer Philip Anderson was one of the thousands of people who moved to Oak Ridge in 1943. He helped plan and manage housing for the workers.

SECRET CITIES

Oak Ridge and other sites looked like cities. The army built houses, schools, hospitals, and shopping centers. But the sites were surrounded by barbed wire and armed guards. They came to be known as secret cities.

Anderson and his family lived in a small two-bedroom house. The army built thousands of houses for Manhattan Project workers. But there were not enough houses for everyone. Some people lived in trailer homes, apartments, or dormitories. Others had to live in small wooden huts called hutments. They had only coal stoves for heat.

Life in the secret cities was not easy. People worked long hours. They were kept apart from their relatives and friends. Cities sometimes lost power and water. Army personnel did what they could to keep people happy. They built theaters and bowling alleys. But some people could not handle living in a secret city. They left the Manhattan Project.

SECURITY

Secrecy was important on the Manhattan Project. Groves did not want the public to learn about the bombs. People could not leave secret cities without the army's approval. The army read and censored workers' mail. Workers were only told what they needed to know to perform their jobs. They could not talk about their

PERSPECTIVES

AFRICAN AMERICAN WORKERS

Roosevelt banned discrimination in the US defense industry in 1941. This paved the way for African Americans to work on military projects. Many came to work on the Manhattan Project. Some were scientists. Others were construction workers or laborers. However, African Americans still had to deal with racial segregation. Racial segregation is the separation of people into groups based on their race. Black workers could not live in the same areas as white workers. They also had separate bathrooms, drinking fountains, and cafeterias.

work with others, even their families.

Groves also feared that spies would steal the army's secrets or destroy its machinery. The army ran background checks on workers before they were hired. Everyone who lived on the sites had to have security badges. Still, some workers broke the secrecy rule. They shared information about the project with spies from the Soviet Union. This information helped the Soviets build their own atomic bomb after the war.

STRAIGHT TO THE SOURCE

William Wilcox Jr. was a chemist. He lived and worked at Oak Ridge. In an interview, he recalled what life was like in the secret city:

> *[Groves] wanted it to have the feel of a normal town. And that's why they did such a beautiful job on the layout of the community. People were relatively happy—it was a great place to raise kids. They had neighborhood schools and neighborhood shopping centers. There were buses here, loads of them, but most people could walk to a shopping center where there was a grocery store, beauty shop, barbershop, laundry—little strips, twelve of them all around the town. And there were nine elementary schools so most kids could walk to school. So the town was really a remarkable place.*

Source: Atomic Heritage Foundation. "William J. Wilcox, Jr.'s Interview (2006)." *Voices of the Manhattan Project*, 2013, manhattanprojectvoices.org. Accessed 23 Sept. 2019.

CONSIDER YOUR AUDIENCE

Adapt this passage for a different audience, such as your friends. Write a blog post conveying this same information for the new audience. How does your post differ from the original text and why?

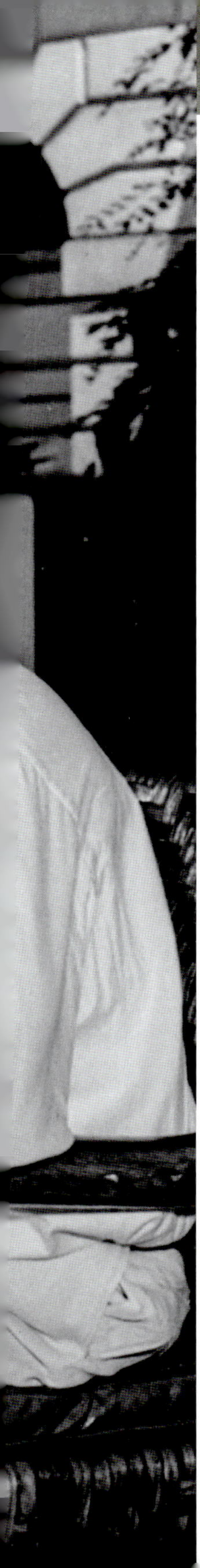

CHAPTER FIVE

DROPPING THE BOMBS

Roosevelt had approved the building of the atomic bombs. But he would not make the decision to use them. He died on April 12, 1945. Vice President Harry Truman became president. Truman chose to use the bombs. He believed this was the only way to win the war.

The two bombs were ready by the summer of 1945. The designers of the uranium bomb were certain it would work. So the army decided not to test that bomb.

Roosevelt, *right*, did not tell Truman, *left*, about the Manhattan Project. Truman learned about the project after Roosevelt's death.

But the implosion device on the plutonium bomb was complicated. Not everyone was sure it would work. It had to be tested.

THE TRINITY TEST

The plutonium bomb was moved from Los Alamos to an army air base in Alamogordo. Physicist J. Robert Oppenheimer called the location Trinity. Trinity became the code name for the atomic bomb test.

The bomb was ready to test on the morning of July 16. A worker triggered the bomb. It exploded. Observers saw a blinding flash of light. They felt a blast of hot air. The heat from the explosion melted the desert sand into glass. The test was a success.

SECOND THOUGHTS

After the Trinity test, some scientists became uneasy. They did not want their work to kill innocent people. The day after the test, Szilard wrote a letter to Truman. He asked Truman not to use the bomb. Several scientists signed the letter. Some scientists

The Trinity test explosion created a giant fireball 2,000 feet (600 m) wide.

instead wanted to drop the bomb over an unpopulated area to demonstrate its power. They thought this might scare the Japanese into surrendering. Other people came up with alternative options too. The US military could invade Japan or block its ports. But Truman had made up his mind. He planned to drop the bomb on a Japanese city.

On July 26, the Allies sent Japan a message. They demanded that Japan surrender. They threatened destruction if the Japanese refused to do so. But they did not mention the atomic bomb. The Japanese did not surrender.

PERSPECTIVES

GERMANY'S PROGRAM

In 1939, the German government formed a program to develop an atomic bomb. But the government did not have enough resources. It eventually abandoned the project. When Allied forces invaded Germany in 1945, they looked for signs of the project. They found nothing to suggest that the Germans were ever close to building a bomb. Physicist Joseph Rotblat worked on the Manhattan Project. He later said in an interview, "It became clearer gradually that the Germans [were] not going to make the bomb. The only reason really why I worked on the bomb was because of the fear of the Germans."

LITTLE BOY

At 8:15 a.m. on August 6, the United States dropped Little Boy on Hiroshima. The city was home to about 330,000 people. Approximately 80,000 died in an instant. Everything within 1 mile (2 km) of the explosion was reduced to rubble. Thousands of people would die from injuries or radiation sickness in the following days.

Later that day, Truman made an announcement over the radio. He told Americans that the United States had dropped an atomic bomb on Hiroshima. The secret was out. Only then did most

RADIATION

Radiation is energy in motion. People are exposed to radiation every day in the form of sunlight. It is harmless in low doses. But atomic bombs give off a lot of radiation when they explode. High doses of radiation can kill living cells. Radiation from the atomic bombs burned people and made them sick. Some people's hair fell out. In time, some developed cancer. Thousands of Japanese people who survived the bomb blasts later died from radiation sickness or cancer.

people on the Manhattan Project learn what they had worked on. Some of them cheered when they heard the news. They were proud of the role they had played in ending the war. Others felt guilty that their work had killed thousands of civilians.

FAT MAN

Three days after the bombing of Hiroshima, the Japanese had still not surrendered. By then, the US military had assembled Fat Man. On August 9, the United States dropped the bomb on Nagasaki. Approximately 263,000 people lived in the city. The explosion instantly killed as many as 40,000 people. It injured many more. Much of the city was destroyed.

The US military prepared to build more atomic bombs in case Japan did not surrender. Groves estimated that the military could have more bombs ready by the end of September. But more bombs were not needed. On August 14, Japan surrendered. World War II was over.

Oak Ridge residents celebrate the end of World War II in August 1945.

LEGACY

The atomic bombs killed thousands of people. But this strategy may have saved many lives by ending World War II early. People continue to debate whether using atomic bombs was the right decision.

The Manhattan Project's legacy is complicated. The Los Alamos National Laboratory still develops military weapons that help protect the nation. The technology used to make the atom bomb is now used to create clean energy. Much of the energy people produce releases pollution that causes climate change. Climate change is a change in Earth's temperatures and weather patterns. Clean energy does not contribute to climate change.

However, the Manhattan Project's success inspired other countries to develop nuclear weapons. The number of countries with these weapons continues to grow. This increases the possibility of nuclear war. Today, there are enough nuclear weapons to kill millions of people. But the United Nations and other groups that promote world peace are working to reduce this threat. They hope to one day see a world free of nuclear weapons.

STRAIGHT TO THE SOURCE

Philip Anderson Jr. was a young boy when he and his family moved to Oak Ridge. His father worked on the Manhattan Project. Years later, he described how he felt when he learned about the Hiroshima bombing:

> *I knew that something very, very important was going on, even though it was a secret. . . . I didn't know what the secret was until the bomb was dropped. Then I realized what was going on, as everybody did. And I was elated. . . . There were gatherings everywhere, cheering crowds, and it was a great celebration. . . . The war had to be ended. It was a painful end for the people who were our enemies, but they were our enemies, and they would have killed our people if we had not killed them.*

Source: Atomic Heritage Foundation. "Philip S. Anderson, Jr.'s Interview." *Voices of the Manhattan Project*, 2019, manhattanprojectvoices.org. Accessed 24 Sept. 2019.

CHANGING MINDS

Anderson suggests that using the atomic bomb was the right decision. Take a position on whether you think dropping the atomic bomb was the right decision. Then imagine your friend has the opposite opinion. Try to convince your friend of your view, using evidence to support your argument.

IMPORTANT DATES

December 1938
German scientists split a uranium atom.

September 1, 1939
Germany invades Poland. This invasion marks the beginning of World War II.

June 1941
Roosevelt creates the Office of Scientific Research and Development (OSRD).

August 1942
The US Army begins the Manhattan Project.

May 7, 1945
Germany surrenders, ending the war in Europe.

July 16, 1945
The Trinity atomic bomb test takes place in Alamogordo, New Mexico.

August 6, 1945
The United States drops Little Boy on Hiroshima.

August 9, 1945
The United States drops Fat Man on Nagasaki.

August 14, 1945
Japan surrenders, ending World War II.

STOP AND THINK

Tell the Tale

Chapter One of this book describes the Trinity test. Imagine you were one of the scientists or engineers who witnessed the test. Write 200 words about the experience. How might this event influence your feelings about the atomic bomb?

Surprise Me

Chapter Four discusses what life was like for people who worked on the Manhattan Project. After reading this chapter, what two or three facts about the workers' lives did you find most surprising? Write a few sentences about each fact. Why did you find each fact surprising?

Dig Deeper

After reading this book, what questions do you still have about the Manhattan Project? With an adult's help, find a few reliable sources that can help you answer your questions. Write a paragraph about what you learned.

Take a Stand

General Leslie Groves forced people from their homes so he could build factories for the Manhattan Project. Do you think this was the right decision? Why or why not? Do you think Groves could have come up with a different solution?

GLOSSARY

atom
the smallest individual part that makes up a substance

censor
to remove or suppress information

civilian
someone who is not a member of a country's military

discrimination
the unjust treatment of a person or group based on race or other perceived differences

implosion
a process that occurs when something collapses inward

mass
a collection of something that holds or clings together

oppress
to control or rule over people in a harsh and cruel way

persecution
the act of treating people cruelly because of their religion, race, or other characteristics

technician
someone who operates technical equipment such as radios and laboratory instruments

ONLINE RESOURCES

To learn more about the Manhattan Project, visit our free resource websites below.

Core Library CONNECTION
FREE! COMMON CORE MULTIMEDIA RESOURCES

Visit **abdocorelibrary.com** or scan this QR code for free Common Core resources for teachers and students, including vetted activities, multimedia, and booklinks, for deeper subject comprehension.

Booklinks NONFICTION NETWORK
FREE! ONLINE NONFICTION RESOURCES

Visit **abdobooklinks.com** or scan this QR code for free additional online weblinks for further learning. These links are routinely monitored and updated to provide the most current information available.

LEARN MORE

Conley, Kate. *World War II through the Eyes of Franklin Delano Roosevelt*. Abdo Publishing, 2016.

Lanier, Wendy H. *Life during World War II*. Abdo Publishing, 2015.

INDEX

About the Author

Ryan Gale is an author from Minnesota. He enjoys writing about history for both children and adults.